Kyle Kitten
and Friends

Short Stories, Fuzzy Animals and Life Lessons

Karma for Kids Books

Norma MacDonald

Kyle Kitten and Friends
Short Stories, Fuzzy Animals and Life Lessons

Copyright © 2018 Norma MacDonald

First Edition

Published by: Find Your Way Publishing, Inc.
PO BOX 667
Norway, ME 04268 U.S.A.
www.findyourwaypublishing.com

ISBN-13: 978-1-945290-13-8

ISBN-10: 1-945290-13-7

Library of Congress Control Number: 2018934794

Printed in the United States of America.

Dedication

This book is dedicated to all the people trying to make the world a better place. You are making a positive difference!

"Radiate and give love, and love comes back to you." ~ Unknown

"You always reap what you sow; there is no shortcut." ~ Stephen Covey

Table of Contents

About This Book

Welcome to our Karma for Kids Book Series. We are very grateful that you picked up this book. We believe together we can make a positive difference, one child at a time. We strive to instill important life lessons in the lives of young children. We are firm believers that we reap what we sow and think that if this simple lesson is taught to children at a young age, their lives have the potential to be absolutely amazing.

We once knew a dog named Karma. She was a beautiful, yellow Labrador retriever. It wasn't until after she passed, at 11 years old, that we realized just how fitting her name really was.

Karma is indeed a retriever.

Whatever we threw out, Karma was always happy to bring it back to us. It didn't matter what it was, she always brought it back. If we threw out garbage, she'd bring it back without question. If we threw out the most beautiful dog toy, she'd bring it back. It's the same in life. Whatever you send out, is what you will get back. Guaranteed. Every time. Our Karma for Kids Book Series hopes to instill this easy-to-understand lesson into the lives of children at a young age. The Universe wants to happily bring you all that your heart desires, and it will, effortlessly. But first, you've got to throw out what you want it to bring back to you so that it can! Have fun with this and watch the magic happen. God bless!

Find all of Norma MacDonald's Karma for Kids Books at Amazon.com.

For more of our Karma for Kids books please visit us at:

www.karmaforkidsbooks.wordpress.com
or
www.findyourwaypublishing.com

Other books that we recommend to help children learn important life lessons:

The Panda Family Relies on Each Other: Short Stories, Fuzzy Animals, and Life Lessons by Norma MacDonald

Matt the African Meerkat and Friends: Short Stories, Fuzzy Animals, and Life Lessons by Norma MacDonald

Kimmie Koala and Friends: Short Stories, Fuzzy Animals, and Life Lessons by Norma MacDonald

Cranky Crocodile Saves the Day: Short Stories, Fuzzy Animals, and Life Lessons by Norma MacDonald

The Many Adventures of Peppy the Emperor Penguin: Short Stories, Fuzzy Animals, and Life Lessons by Norma MacDonald

Lucy Llama and Friends: Short Stories, Fuzzy Animals, and Life Lessons by Norma MacDonald

Ethan Eagle and Friends: Short Stories, Fuzzy Animals, and Life Lessons by Norma MacDonald

Billy Brown Bear and Friends: Short Stories, Fuzzy Animals, and Life Lessons by Norma MacDonald

Humble Heron and Friends: Short Stories, Fuzzy Animals, and Life Lessons by Norma MacDonald

Peter Penguin and Friends: Short Stories, Fuzzy Animals and Life Lessons by Norma MacDonald

Guaranteed Success for Kindergarten; 50 Easy Things You Can Do Today! by Marrae Kimball

Guaranteed Success for Grade School; 50 Easy Things You Can Do Today! by Marrae Kimball

The Secret Combination to Middle School: Real Advice from Real Kids, Ideas for Success, and Much More! by Marrae Kimball

Kyle Kitten and Friends

Short Stories, Fuzzy Animals, and Life Lessons

Karma for Kids Books

Norma MacDonald

Chapter One

Every day, during class, the students get a break to play. It is important for the students to use their imagination while playing with toys and to get exercise while running around. Usually, the class splits up and the girls play with the dolls and the boys run around and play sports.

Susie Squirrel and Penny Pigeon are best friends and always play with dolls together.

Roger Rat and Kyle Kitten are best friends and always play tag with each other.

One day, it was raining outside, and Kyle Kitten did not want to go out and get wet. He decided to go play dolls with Susie Squirrel and Penny Pigeon instead.

"Hi!" Kyle Kitten greeted the two girls. "I think I am going to play with you today so I don't have to go out in the rain. I really don't like getting wet."

Susie Squirrel started to giggle.

Penny Pigeon looked at Kyle Kitten with a very confused expression. "You want to play dolls?"

Kyle Kitten nodded.

"But you're a boy!" Susie Squirrel shouted. She started to laugh even harder and Penny Pigeon joined in.

Kyle Kitten's feelings were hurt. He knew that boys didn't usually play with dolls, but there were no boys inside to play with. He didn't see why he couldn't play with the girls just this one time. Besides, there were some boy dolls to play with, it wasn't like he had to choose a girl doll.

Susie Squirrel and Penny Pigeon went back to playing together and ignored that Kyle Kitten was still standing there. Eventually, he gave up trying to get involved and went and sat quietly at his desk until playtime was over.

When all the boys came back inside they were damp, sweaty, and covered in dirt. Kyle Kitten was glad that he didn't go outside but sad that he wasn't able to have any fun.

"Was it fun inside?" Roger Rat asked.

"Not really," said Kyle Kitten.

"How come?"

"The girls didn't let me play with them."

"Well, I guess playing with dolls is kind of a girl's game, isn't it?" Roger Rat asked.

"Yeah," Kyle Kitten agreed, "but who else would I have played with?"

Roger Rat shrugged.

By the time school was over that day, the sun had come out. All the kids gathered in front of the school waiting to be picked up. A game of tag broke up.

Penny Pigeon ran over to join in.

"You can't play," Roger Rat stopped her.

"Why not?"

"This is a game for boys only."

"I've played tag before!" Penny Pigeon argued.

"Well this kind of tag is a boy's game," Kyle Kitten explained.

The two boys turned and ran off without Penny Pigeon.

Her feelings were hurt and she went over to Susie Squirrel who was sitting under a tree reading a book.

"The boys won't let me play tag!"

"Why not?"

"They said it's a boy's game. That just isn't fair!" Penny Pigeon crossed her wings and pouted.

Kyle Kitten felt a little bit better knowing that he made Penny Pigeon feel left out just like she did to him during play time, but he still didn't understand why girls and boys couldn't play the same games.

He decided to go home and ask his dad.

"Hey dad," Kyle Kitted purred when he got home, "I have a question."

"Okay," said Mr. Kitten.

"Today at school, I didn't want to go outside in the rain, but I couldn't play inside because Susie Squirrel and Penny Pigeon said that the dolls were girl's toys. So, after school, Roger Rat and I didn't let them play tag because it is a boy's game. Who decides what toys and games are for boys and girls?"

"You decide, son."

"But then why couldn't I play with Susie Squirrel and Penny Pigeon?"

"Because they decided that dolls were for girls only. There are no signs on the dolls that say that. Just like there is no rule in tag that says only boys can play. You and your friends just got used to it being that way, you forgot that all toys and games are really for everyone!"

Kyle Kitten thought this made sense. He decided that the next day in school he would explain this to his friends so that if he wanted to stay inside and play dolls, the girls would let him. He also decided that he and Roger Rat should apologize to Penny Pigeon for not letting her play tag since it was a game for everyone. Kyle Kitten felt better knowing that boys and girls were allowed to play the same games together. He couldn't wait to go to school the next day.

When Kyle Kitten got to school, he ran as fast as he could over to his best friend. Roger Rat was gathering the other boys in class to begin a game of tag before the morning bell rang meaning class would begin.

"Kyle Kitten!" Roger Rat exclaimed. "You're just in time for the game to start!"

Kyle Kitten stood confidently and said, "I think we should invite Penny Pigeon and Susie Squirrel to play with us."

Roger Rat and the other boys stood there just looking at Kyle Kitten with surprised looks on their faces. They thought Kyle Kitten was kidding, but he wasn't. He pranced over to where Penny Pigeon and Susie Squirrel were sitting on the steps of the school.

"Do you girls want to come play tag with us?" Kyle Kitten asked.

"I thought tag was only for boys?" Penny Pigeon said with her feathers all ruffled. She was still upset about the day before.

"Well I talked to my dad and I'm sorry about yesterday. I was wrong. My dad said that all games and toys are for whoever wants to play. It doesn't matter if you are a boy or a girl, just as long as you have fun! Everyone can play!"

Penny Pigeon and Susie Squirrel decided they would play tag. The other boys were hesitant at first, but once the game started they found out that they were just as good as the boys. Susie Squirrel was even faster than most of them!

At playtime, later in the day, Kyle Kitten got to play inside and so did some of the other boys while some of the girls went outside to play tag. Realizing that boys and girls are allowed to like the same things made the day one of the most fun days they'd ever had!

Chapter Two

"Class, I have very exciting news!" Miss Butterfly announced to her classroom full of rambunctious students. Her words brought silence to the room as everyone sat on the edge of their seats waiting to hear the news. "Next week we are going on a field trip!"

The class erupted in cheers. Benny Badger was particularly excited. He loved going to new places and seeing new things and being able to spend a day away from his desk. He couldn't wait to find out where they'd be going. He squeezed his eyes shut and wished as hard as he could that they would go to the space museum.

The room grew silent as the students held their breath in anticipation. Miss Butterfly turned to write on the chalkboard. Using big sweeping letters, she wrote R - O - C - K. Benny Badger felt a little let down that it wasn't the space museum, but learning about rocks could be really cool too! Miss Butterfly continued to write. C - L - I - M - B - I - N - G!

"Class, we are going rock climbing! It will be a wonderful way to learn how to work together and encourage each other to step outside our comfort zones. Please return your permission slip by Friday."

The whole class burst out in more cheers. The whole class except for Benny Badger. His heart was pounding a mile a minute. "Rock climbing?!"

He thought, "There's no way I can do that!" You see, Benny Badger was terrified of heights. Anytime he was more than five feet from the ground he would start to sweat and his stomach would knot up. Rock climbing sounded too scary, but he didn't want the class to know that. "Maybe I will fake sick that day." Benny Badger thought. He knew good attendance was important but he was so scared he didn't know what else to do.

When he got home from school, he tossed his backpack into a corner and ran up to his bedroom. He began to plot out his plan of faking sick. He decided that on Sunday he would complain of a headache and then Monday morning the headache would be worse and he would have a cough too. By the time Tuesday rolled around, there was no way his mom would think he was faking it! There was only one problem, Benny Badger forgot to hide the permission slip.

"Benny!" called his dad from downstairs. "You forgot to hang your backpack up again, how many times do I have to tell you not to throw it on the ground?"

"Sorry, dad!"

"And I see you have some homework to do, so come on back down, I'll sign the permission slip once you finish."

Benny Badger's heart sank all the way down into his stomach. He knew that there was no way his dad would let him get out of the field trip because he was always encouraging Benny to try new things and meet new people.

Benny Badger was more of an introvert. That meant that he preferred quiet time alone than being with a bunch of his classmates doing something kind of scary. He went down to do his homework and didn't even put up a fight about the field trip, he put the signed permission slip in his backpack with a sigh.

The week seemed to drag on forever as Benny Badger became more and more nervous every day with anticipation of the rock climbing trip that was approaching.

"Aren't you excited for the field trip?" Kyle Kitten asked him on Friday.

"Definitely," Benny Badger lied.

"I went rock climbing once," Susie Squirrel chimed in. "It was so much fun! I love being up high. It makes everyone on the ground look tiny."

Kyle Kitten laughed. "I bet you will all look like little ants when I look down!"

Benny Badger laughed nervously. He didn't want his friends to know that he was actually terrified about the big trip.

Finally, the day came. Benny Badger went to school with knots in his belly. He boarded the bus with his classmates and sat down next to a window. He hoped that the bus would break down on the way to rock climbing so that they didn't have to go.

All of his classmates were cheering and talking about how excited they were to go rock climbing. It would be the first time for everyone except Susie Squirrel and she was telling everyone how much fun it was going to be. Benny Badger didn't believe her. He looked around to see if anyone else looked nervous and he noticed that Penny Pigeon looked a little scared.

"Hey Penny Pigeon," he called out to her, "come sit by me."

Penny Pigeon sat down next to him but didn't say anything. Usually, she was very talkative, so Benny Badger knew she was nervous too.

"I'm a little bit afraid of heights, but I didn't want anyone to know," he confessed.

"I'm nervous too," Penny Pigeon whispered. "Heights are fine, but I'm not very strong and I don't know if I will be able to make it to the top. I don't want people to laugh at me."

The bus arrived and the class burst into excitement before Benny Badger could respond to

Penny Pigeon. He tried giving her a reassuring smile, but it probably looked like a grimace because his stomach was doing backflips.

They all got off the bus and stood around the instructor who handed out harnesses to everyone and explained some of the rules and safety guidelines. Benny Badger was barely listening because all he could focus on was how much he didn't want to be there. The instructor said that if you didn't feel comfortable climbing, that everyone should at least put on a harness and step up to the wall just to take a small step outside of their comfort zones. Benny Badger felt a little bit better, but then Roger Rat shouted, "Why would anyone not want to climb?" and Benny Badger's heart started racing again. He didn't want his friends to think he was a wimp.

"Okay class," said Miss Butterfly, "I am going to give everyone a number and that will be the order we go in."

Benny Badger prayed that Penny Pigeon would be before him so that if she didn't make it to the top he wouldn't feel as embarrassed when he didn't. Unfortunately, Miss Butterfly started counting at the other end and Benny Badger ended up with the number five and Penny Pigeon was number seven.

The first classmate started to climb and the class cheered them on. Slowly but surely, they made it all the way to the top. The next classmate climbed very quickly to the top. With each climber, Benny Badger got more nervous. The class was being very nice to everyone and cheering them on, but no one had a hard time yet, so Benny Badger didn't know what was to come.

When it was his turn, he took a deep breath and stepped up to the wall. He didn't want to do it, but he knew that he should try.

"Ready?" asked the instructor as they attached the rope to Benny Badger's harness.

He shrugged hesitantly.

"Hey everyone!" the instructor called out. "Some people are a little more nervous than others, so make sure we all continue to encourage and cheer just as loud for everyone, okay?"

"Are you nervous Benny Badger?" Susie Squirrel asked.

Benny Badger nodded hesitantly, he wasn't sure if admitting it was a good idea or a bad idea.

"It's okay!" she said, "I was nervous my first time too, just do your best! Everyone has to start somewhere."

That made Benny Badger feel a little bit better. At least he knew one friend would be supportive.

He took a deep breath and put his foot on the first rock and pushed himself up. He could hear the class cheering and shouting encouraging words. Part of him wanted to say, "that's it" and come down, but the other part of him was saying, "challenge yourself, go a little higher!"

Benny Badger grabbed hold of another rock and climbed a little higher until he was halfway up the wall. "Don't look down. Don't look down." He looked down and was frozen with fear. There was no way he was going to be able to climb any higher.

"I'm ready to come down!" He called out nervously to the instructor.

"Are you sure? Why not just try to go one step higher?" The instructor suggested.

The class cheered. "You can do it, Benny Badger!"

Benny Badger took a deep breath and looked up. The top seemed so much farther away now. He looked down. The ground looked a lot more pleasing. "Yes, "he said, "I'm ready to come down."

The instructor began to lower him to the ground and his heart started to race again. He was the first one to not go all the way to the top. Would anyone make fun of him for it? But then he realized that it didn't really matter because he was proud of himself for even giving it a try. He made it a lot higher than he thought he would.

Luckily, the class was very nice to him.

"You did such a good job for being afraid of heights," said Penny Pigeon.

"I didn't even know you were scared!" Kyle Kitten chimed in. "You didn't even show it and it's cool you gave it a try!"

Benny Badger realized that there was no reason to worry about what his friends would think. All he needed to do was step outside his comfort zone and challenge himself and his true friends would support him. He was very proud of what he accomplished and glad that he hadn't pretended to be sick. He couldn't wait to go home to tell his dad about the best field trip ever!

Chapter Three

After a long day at school, all Roger Rat wanted to do was play with his toys or run around outside or watch TV. Every day he would try to sneak inside his house and tiptoe up to his room to play before his mom realized he was home. When she knew he was home, she always made him do his homework first; before he could play or do anything fun. Roger Rat really disliked homework. He didn't understand why they had to do more school work at home after they had just spent the whole day learning.

"Roger Rat, do you have homework today?"

He knew better than to lie to his mom, so he trudged over to his backpack and pulled out his homework folder. Today he had to do a math worksheet and a vocabulary worksheet.

He sped through the vocabulary worksheet, not even reading the words. He just circled random answers and hoped for the best. Math was a little harder to speed through because Miss Butterfly expected everyone to show their work on how they got their answers. The first couple of questions were easy, but then they started to get more complicated and Roger Rat couldn't remember if he was supposed to add or divide first. He didn't want to waste time looking up how to do it in his math book, so he made up his own rules.

"Done!" he called to his mom.

She came into his room to check that he really completed the homework. He held up both worksheets with the answers filled in and then showed her the empty homework folder to prove there was nothing else to do.

"Good job. Dinner will be ready in an hour."

Roger Rat ran over to turn on his TV. He finished his homework just in time to watch his favorite show.

The next day Miss Butterfly collected all the homework and then started teaching new things. Roger Rat tried his best to pay attention, but he was having a hard time following some of the new math rules. He was still confused about the order of adding, subtracting, multiplying, and dividing. He thought that Miss Butterfly would go over the homework, but she jumped right into teaching about fractions.

At recess, Roger Rat asked his friends if they thought fractions were too hard.

"They're a little bit confusing, but I'm sure the homework tonight will help us understand it better," said Kyle Kitten.

"I think they're easy!" Susie Squirrel said.

"That's because you're good at math," said Benny Badger.

Roger Rat hoped that Kyle Kitten was right that the homework would help. When he got home from school he opened his homework folder to look at the math homework. Today he had a whole packet to complete. He groaned, feeling annoyed at how long this was going to take him.

The first few questions were tricky because he still didn't know all the rules, but he gave it his best guess. Roger Rat was watching the clock because he didn't want to miss his TV show, so he didn't want to waste time on problems that he already knew confused him.

On the second page of the math packet, the questions with fractions started. Some of them were easy, he knew that half of two was one and that a quarter of one hundred was twenty-five.

"Maybe fractions aren't that bad," he thought.

But then he got to a question that required him to add two fractions together where the denominator, or the bottom number, was not the same! Feeling very frustrated, Roger Rat gave up, he filled in all the blanks with random fractions and didn't bother showing his work. There were only ten minutes before his show started, and he didn't want to risk missing the beginning.

"Do you have homework today?" his mom came in to ask.

"Already done," Roger Rat told her. He opened his folder to show her but didn't flip to the second page because she might notice that he didn't show his work.

"Wow, good job honey!" his mom said. "Usually I have to remind you. I'm so proud of you."

Roger Rat didn't feel proud. He felt discouraged. More and more math was being taught in class, but he couldn't keep up. He hoped that Miss Butterfly would review with them in school the next day so that he didn't have to review himself after school and waste time.

The next day Miss Butterfly collected the homework packets and passed out a different packet. "Class, we are going to have a pop quiz today. It shouldn't take you too long, just a review of some things we've learned with a bonus question on fractions."

Everyone started writing furiously on their quizzes. Roger Rat looked around and everyone seemed to be having no problem calculating the answers except him. He didn't know if he should multiply before adding and dividing or add first or divide first. There were too many numbers and too many parts of the question.

When he got to the bonus question, he didn't even try it. There was no way he could figure out something that he didn't have any idea how to do. At least it was a bonus question, that meant he wouldn't lose any points for not doing it.

Miss Butterfly collected the tests and released the class to recess while she began to grade them.

"That was so easy!" Roger Rat heard someone say. That made him mad. He didn't like being bad at things when his friends were so good at them. He went to the bathroom to try and calm down and forget about the quiz before playing with his friends.

On his way to the bathroom, Miss Butterfly pulled him aside.

"Roger Rat, your homework grades lately and your quiz today were not very good. Do you need some extra help with your math?"

"I just have a hard time remembering the order of how to do things and so when we started learning fractions, I couldn't pay attention because I was still trying to learn the last lesson."

"Well that's why your homework is so important," she said, "you need to practice."

"But homework is a waste of time. If we already learn it in class, I don't want to do it again at home."

"You like to play soccer, right?" Miss Butterfly asked.

"Yes..." Roger Rat answered confused. What in the world did soccer have to do with his math homework?

"When you first started to play soccer, how far could you kick the ball?"

Roger Rat laughed, thinking about his first time trying to kick a soccer ball. "The first time I tried to kick the ball I completely missed."

"And how far can you kick it now?" Miss Butterfly asked.

"I can kick it almost all the way across the field!" Roger Rat loved to brag about how good he was at soccer. He was the best in the whole school.

"How did you go from not being able to kick the ball to being the best at it?"

"Practice," Roger Rat said, "Practice makes perfect!"

"Well, that's what homework is there for," Miss Butterfly explained. "If you do not practice something new, you won't ever completely learn it. I know that it feels like a waste of time because it might not be as fun as soccer practice, but the only way to really learn your math is to practice."

That made a lot of sense to Roger Rat, he had never thought of it that way before. Whenever he has soccer practice, he has to miss some of the TV shows that he likes, but he doesn't care because soccer is fun for him, but it's still practice. Just because homework isn't as fun as soccer doesn't mean it isn't important.

"If you need some extra help, you can stay after class and I'll give you some more direction," Miss Butterfly offered.

Roger Rat nodded and thanked her.

When the school bell rang at the end of the day and all his friends ran out to the schoolyard, Roger Rat stayed behind to go over some math problems with Miss Butterfly. She explained everything that confused him and showed him where to look in his math book if he ever had questions while doing his homework. He felt a lot better.

"Why don't you stay after class tomorrow and retake your quiz."

Roger Rat was so happy that Miss Butterfly was going to give him another chance. Now that he understood the importance of homework, he knew that he would do just fine. Miss Butterfly handed Roger Rat a packet of math problems to take home with him that night.

"This is just for you to practice, no need to turn it in tomorrow."

When Roger Rat got home that night he did all of his normal homework with no problem. He only had to check his math book one time. The clock showed that there were five minutes before his TV show came on. Instead of playing with his toys for those five minutes, Roger Rat decided to keep practicing his math. He got so into it that he lost track of time and finished the math packet instead of watching TV. "Oh well," he thought, "I'll just watch the rerun during the weekend."

He stuffed his homework and practice packet back into his backpack and climbed into bed to go to sleep.

The next day in school Roger Rat found it much easier to follow along in class. "I know the answer because that was on the homework!" he would think every time there was a problem he easily understood. When decimals got added in, he had no problem figuring out how to do them because he already understood everything else.

After school ended he stuck around to retake the quiz that he had failed and he ended up getting every answer correct- even the bonus question!

Roger Rat was happy that he was doing better in school. He still disliked homework and would much rather watch TV, but at least now he realized why it was so important to do.

Chapter Four

Every morning Susie Squirrel's mom woke her up with a light kiss on the forehead and a whisper of "good morning, my sweet squirrel."

Susie Squirrel thought it was the best way in the whole world to be woken up for school. Her mom would help her pick out her outfit and then while Susie Squirrel got dressed her mom would go to the kitchen and prepare a bowl of cereal.

As Susie Squirrel sat at the table eating her cereal her mom brushed her hair very gently. Susie

Squirrel loved having her hair done by her mom. It always gave her tickling chills and goosebumps. Having her mother around to give her affection was the best feeling and Susie Squirrel couldn't think of a better way to get ready for school.

Finally, when it was time to go catch the bus, her mom always gave her a big tight hug and a kiss right on the top of her head. "I love you Susie Squirrel. Have a wonderful day at school!"

Susie Squirrel would then get on the bus feeling warm and happy, with her mother's loving hug still lingering and the chills from getting her hair brushed still running down her back. When she got to school she wanted to make sure all her friends felt just as happy as she did.

Penny Pidgeon woke up to the sound of her father feeding her baby brother. She would rub her eyes, and wish for just one more minute of peaceful sleep. Her brother would cry out between each bite of breakfast, thinking that there wouldn't be any more food for him, but there always was.

Penny Pidgeon got out of her bed and hopped across the nest to join in on breakfast.

"Good morning, Penny, I hope you slept well." Her father always greeted her the same way. It made up for being woken up by her brother's cries, knowing that her father's caring voice would be there to greet her.

After she ate, she hopped back over to her space to straighten up her hair, gather her things, and leave.

"Bye, Dad!"

"Love you, Penny Pidgeon!"

"Love you, too!"

Penny Pidgeon got on the bus thinking about how lucky her brother was that he was still young enough to need their father's help in the morning. She missed the days that her dad would feed her breakfast, but loved knowing that she was a big girl now and that her dad trusted her to get ready all by herself. It was a very exciting way to start the morning.

Susie Squirrel and Penny Pidgeon met each other under their favorite tree to walk into school together.

"Hi, Penny Pidgeon!" Susie Squirrel shouted when she saw her best friend get off the bus. She ran over and wrapped her up in a big hug.

Penny Pidgeon squirmed out of Susie Squirrel's grip, feeling confused about why she was getting a hug. "Are you okay Susie Squirrel?"

"Of course, I'm okay! Are you?" Susie Squirrel didn't understand why Penny Pidgeon didn't hug her back. She was worried that she had done something wrong.

"I'm okay."

The two friends walked into the classroom together and greeted the rest of their friends who were already inside.

The lesson that day seemed to go on forever. Penny Pidgeon kept looking at the clock waiting for it to hit noon so that they could eat lunch and go play outside. Susie Squirrel passed the time by drawing pictures along the border of her notebook pages.

Finally, the bell rang. Susie Squirrel jumped up and cheered, "Finally!" She was so excited, she wrapped up her best friend in another hug.

Again, Penny Pidgeon squirmed away.

"Are you mad at me?" Susie Squirrel asked. She couldn't understand why Penny Pidgeon wasn't hugging her back. Hugs were the best thing in the whole world. They made her feel happy and loved. She just wanted Penny Pidgeon to feel the same way because they were best friends.

"I'm not mad at you."

"Then why do you keep backing up when I try to give you a hug?"

"I just don't really like hugs that much. They are only for really special moments and recess happens every day, it's not that special."

Susie Squirrel was so surprised. "I love hugs! My mom gives me a big one every morning before I leave for school. It makes me really happy, so I thought it would make you happy too."

"I am happy!" Penny Pidgeon said, "My family just doesn't hug that often, we just use our words to tell each other we love each other."

The two friends told each other about how they begin each morning. One with lots of hugs and kisses and one with independence and words of affirmation. They decided that one wasn't better than the other because both mornings felt the same to them. As long as they felt loved and happy, it didn't really matter. Susie Squirrel learned that she should save hugs for Penny Pidgeon for special occasions and Penny Pidgeon learned that sometimes it's okay to hug just to hug. Susie Squirrel said, "Maybe I'll do my own hair and get my own breakfast tomorrow." And Penny Pidgeon said, "And maybe I will give my dad a hug before I leave next time." They learned that there are different ways to do things and they can all be good. But the most important lesson both friends learned was that asking questions and talking about their feelings they got things out in the open so that no one's feelings were hurt by mistake.

Chapter Five

Kyle Kitten loved when his parents had parties. Everyone always had so much fun. The neighbors would come over and sit around eating cheese and snacks and some of the grownups enjoyed a little catnip. After a while, some of them would start acting really silly. Kyle Kitten watched as his normally serious neighbor would giggle and laugh louder than normal. It wasn't something they did every day and there was a sense of mystery knowing that catnip had the power to make the normally mature grownups act like children.

Kyle Kitten knew the rules though, you had to be a grown up before you were allowed to eat catnip. He learned about it in school. The teachers taught that if you weren't done growing, it could be very dangerous and make your brain not work as well.

He learned about it from his parents. They told him that catnip might seem like something cool and fun, but that there are rules and laws for a reason. And that adults have to be smart and very responsible because others could get seriously injured or hurt, otherwise. For as long as Kyle Kitten could remember his parents would share stories about others who didn't follow the rules and the unfortunate consequences that happened because of their decisions.

He even learned about it from complete strangers. Like the one time he saw a stray cat who was acting very strange. "Must've had too much catnip" he heard someone say.

Kyle Kitten knew the rules. He knew that catnip was bad for you and he knew that it was only for adults, but when he walked into the kitchen and saw the catnip on the table, with no one else around, he became more curious than ever. If it made adults act silly, he wanted to know what it would make him act like.

As his parents were saying goodbye to their guests at the front door, he snuck a small amount of catnip and ran to his bedroom. He sat on his bed and watched TV wondering when he would start to feel silly.

It happened without him really noticing. He was watching cartoons and then all of a sudden, he was laughing more than usual at the jokes. He stomach felt kind of tight, and it made him want to move around. He started to roll around on his bed. The neat soft blankets started to get all messed up. He thought about how silly he must look just rolling back and forth on his bed.

"Kyle Kitten?"

He heard his mom's voice on the other side of the door. He jumped at the sound of it and sat up, trying his best to act normal. The door opened and his mom poked her head into his room.

"It's getting late," she said, "you should probably be getting ready to go to sleep."

Kyle Kitten nodded. He was too nervous to speak, nervous that she would know he snuck some catnip. His nerves made the silly feeling turn into a very bad and scary feeling. His mom left and Kyle Kitten got into his bed. He stretched out on his back, trying to stretch out the nauseous feeling in his belly, but it wouldn't go away. He felt a bit dizzy, but finally, Kyle Kitten was able to fall asleep. When he woke up the next morning the stomach ache was gone.

He couldn't wait to get to school and tell his friends that he tried catnip. They would think he was so cool. He thought they would be impressed with him.

They weren't.

"Kyle Kitten that is so stupid!" Benny Badger said when he found out. "You know how bad catnip is for you, I don't know why you would be curious!"

"I agree," said Susie Squirrel.

Roger Rat nodded along.

"Just don't do it again," Benny Badger lectured, "or else you'll fry your brain and fail out of school."

Kyle Kitten thought his friends were overreacting. He had only eaten a little bit of catnip. His parents and their friends ate more and they were fine. Feeling determined to prove his friends wrong, he decided that when he got home from school he was going to sneak a little bit more catnip.

During class, he couldn't stop thinking about how he was going to get it. He would need to make sure his parents were distracted so that he would not get caught. Eventually, the end of the day bell rang and Kyle Kitten ran out to the bus. He sat in the first seat so that he could get off quicker.

When he got home, Kyle Kitten was anxious and he threw his backpack down harder than usual.

He accidentally knocked over his mother's favorite vase filled with colorful flowers. The vase shattered on the ground spilling water and flowers everywhere.

His mother rushed into the room and ordered him to go get paper towels to clean up the mess he had made while she began picking up the flowers one by one and organizing them back into a beautiful arrangement.

Kyle Kitten's heart was racing as he walked into the kitchen. He knew his parents kept the catnip in the back of the snack cabinet which was two cabinets away from where the paper towels were. He slowly opened the cabinet and reached in carefully, trying not to knock anything else over or make any sounds. He found the catnip, ate a little more than the night before, and put it back. He grabbed the paper towels and ran back out to his mom.

"Here are the paper towels. Sorry I knocked over your flowers, I just have a lot of homework and was so frustrated about it that I guess I set my backpack down too hard." He lied.

"Well, then you better go get started on your homework while I clean this mess up."

Kyle Kitten trotted up the stairs to his bedroom and opened his homework folder. He didn't really have that much, but now he had more time to sit in his room with the door closed.

About halfway through his worksheet, he started feeling weird. The letters on his homework seemed to dance around on the page and he got that same tight feeling in his stomach. He started to laugh a little. "If catnip makes you laugh, it can't be as bad as they say," he thought to himself.

He saw his favorite ball out of the corner of his eye and started to chase it around the room kicking and swatting at it mid-stride. He was having a blast. About an hour later, he was feeling less silly. His stomach started hurting again and he had a slight headache. He drank some water.

"Dinner time!"

Kyle Kitten shoved his homework back into his backpack, drank some more water, and took a deep breath to try to act normal for dinner.

"You seem so tired, you really must have had a lot of homework," his mom observed.

Kyle Kitten nodded.

He ate his dinner in silence, worried that if he spoke, his mom would know what he did. His dad seemed too busy reading the newspaper that he probably wouldn't have noticed if Kyle Kitten didn't come down for dinner at all.

Kyle Kitten ate as much as he could without making his stomach hurt more and then excused himself to go upstairs. He got into his bed and fell asleep right away.

In the morning, Kyle Kitten woke up with a very bad headache. He went to drink water, but his bowl was empty because he drank so much the night before. When he got out of bed, his head hurt even more.

"How did you sleep, son?" Kyle Kitten's dad asked when he came downstairs. It sounded like he was screaming.

Kyle Kitten must have winced at the sound of his dad's voice.

"Are you okay?"

"Yeah," Kyle Kitten said, "I just have a bit of a headache." He ate his breakfast and trudged off to school.

Miss Butterfly asked everyone to hand their homework in, and Kyle Kitten reached into his backpack to grab the worksheet. When he took it out of the folder he noticed that he only finished half of it. He had no other choice but to turn it in.

During the lesson, Kyle Kitten couldn't pay attention. His headache still hadn't gone away. It took everything in him to stay awake and pay attention. When the lunch bell rang, Kyle Kitten had to cover his ears. With his headache, every noise seemed louder than normal.

As Kyle Kitten was leaving his desk to go to the cafeteria, Miss Butterfly intercepted him. "Can you wait and see me after class?" she asked.

Once everyone was out of the classroom, Kyle Kitten walked slowly over to his teacher's desk. It was never a good feeling having to talk to the teacher alone, especially with how he felt this particular day.

"Why didn't you finish your homework?" Miss Butterfly inquired.

"I had a bad headache last night and just fell asleep. Sorry."

"Why don't you come back here during recess to finish it?" Miss Butterfly offered. Kyle Kitten was thankful that Miss Butterfly was so understanding, but felt very guilty that he had just lied to her and gotten a second chance because of it.

After school, Kyle Kitten's friends all wanted to know what he had done to miss recess. Usually, Miss Butterfly made the children who acted out in class stay inside, but Kyle Kitten was very well behaved.

"She was letting me finish my homework," he explained.

"Why didn't you finish your homework?" Penny Pidgeon asked.

"Uhhh... I just had a headache and went to sleep." Kyle Kitten had a very guilty look on his face.

"Did you steal some of your parent's catnip again?! If so, you're lucky something worse didn't happen, Kyle Kitten!"

He didn't know what to say to explain himself, so Kyle Kitten just put his head down and shuffled his feet.

His friends reprimanded him over and over again and he swore never to eat catnip ever again. He didn't like how it made him feel, he didn't like that it made him forgetful, and he didn't like that his friends all knew better. Kyle Kitten knew that he let curiosity get the best of him, but he swore to always listen to his parents and teachers from that moment on. He also decided that he would go home and tell his parents the truth.

Chapter Six

Susie Squirrel was a very lucky girl. She had a mom and dad who loved her. She had a big home and comfortable bed. Her friends were all very nice and lived nearby. Her school was close enough to walk to and her neighborhood was very safe. Susie Squirrel was indeed lucky, but she did not know just how lucky.

One day in school, Miss Butterfly wrote a big letter 'P' on the chalkboard. She turned to the class and asked for some adjectives that start with P to describe themselves.

61

"Popular!"

"Pretty!"

"Perfect!"

"Polite!"

Miss Butterfly wrote all of the words on the board as the class shouted them out. She nodded along as she wrote them. Finally, she motioned for them to stop and the room fell silent.

"What about this word," she paused and began writing on the board again. She said out loud as she wrote it, "privileged?"

She turned back to the class to see confused expressions on everyone's face. No one seemed to know what the word meant, so they weren't sure if it described them or not.

"Being privileged means that you have some sort of special right. For example, we are all privileged to live in the same home every night, but some people are homeless. Can anyone think of other examples of how we are all privileged?"

Susie Squirrel raised her hand. When Miss Butterfly called on her said, "Is it a privilege that our school gives us crayons, pencils, and paper, while some other schools can't afford to do that?"

"Good example," said Miss Butterfly. "Anyone else?"

Roger Rat called out, "I think because I have two parents that work, I am able to play travel soccer which is an expensive sport while some of my friends can't. Is that privileged?"

"Indeed, it is, thank you for sharing!"

Other students shared examples of their different privileges. All of a sudden, a new mood was in the classroom. Everyone started to feel grateful for the things they took for granted.

"Miss Butterfly," Susie Squirrel called out to her teacher. "I don't think it's fair that I am more privileged than others in the world."

"I am so happy you shared that Susie Squirrel," Miss Butterfly said. "Because we are all going to volunteer at a soup kitchen this weekend to give back to those who might be less privileged than we are."

The class wasn't sure how to react. Usually getting out of the classroom was fun, but they had never volunteered before. No one knew if it would be fun or boring or hard. They would just have to wait and see.

The day of the volunteer project, Susie Squirrel felt nervous. She didn't know what to expect or who she might encounter. She had heard of homeless people before. Weren't they dirty and kind of scary?

"Welcome to Brier Kitchen! My name is Harold Hippo!" The class stood around looking up to Harold. He was gigantic and his voice was deep and rumbling like thunder. "There are a lot of homeless folks out there and a lot of folks who can't afford groceries to make dinner every night, can you imagine?"

Susie Squirrel couldn't imagine that. Her parents always had a warm dinner for her, and a filling lunch for school, and a nutritious breakfast to start her day on the right foot. Thinking about not having enough money to buy food was scary.

"Well, here at Brier Kitchen," Harold Hippo continued, "We believe that anyone can experience hard times. It could happen to any of us, therefore, it is up to those of us who have the privilege of buying food to give back to our community. So, every night we serve up a nice hot dinner for anyone who needs it!"

He then assigned everyone to different tasks. Some would scoop mashed potatoes, some would pour cups of juice, some oversaw cleaning off the tables, and some were in charge of greeting those who came in. Susie Squirrel was surprised to see how many people came to Brier Kitchen for dinner.

She realized that her parent's hard work and love for her was something that she should be thankful for. When she got home from the volunteer trip she felt a sense of pride knowing that she helped out and a new appreciation for her comfortable life.

"Did you know that we are privileged?" she asked her parents.

They smiled at her and said yes.

"We should use that to help other people. Can we volunteer at Brier Kitchen as a family?"

Susie Squirrel's mom and dad wrapped her up in a huge hug. They were very proud of their daughter for wanting to help people who didn't have as much as she did.

Will You Help Us Out?

Would you please consider leaving reviews for our books? It doesn't have to be long and will only take a minute. It would mean a lot and help us get the word out, to other children, as well. Thank you so much!

AFTERWORD

Thanks again for picking up this book! You are participating in making our world a better place to live and grow. When children learn that they will always get back what they give, they will start to navigate their lives in incredible ways. When you give a smile, and make someone's heart feel lighter and happier, because of it, you can be sure that you will receive something in the near future that will make your heart happier as well. When you do something kind for someone, you can be sure that someone will do something kind for you in the coming days ahead. It is truly amazing how it works! Have fun with it and enjoy!

For more of our *Karma for Kids Books* please visit us at:

www.karmaforkidsbooks.wordpress.com
or
www.findyourwaypublishing.com

Find Norma MacDonald and her books online at Amazon.com.

The Panda Family Relies on Each Other: Short Stories, Fuzzy Animals, and Life Lessons

Matt the African Meerkat and Friends: Short Stories, Fuzzy Animals, and Life Lessons

The Many Adventures of Peppy the Emperor Penguin: Short Stories, Fuzzy Animals, and Life Lessons

Kimmie Koala and Friends: Short Stories, Fuzzy Animals, and Life Lessons

Cranky Crocodile Saves the Day: Short Stories, Fuzzy Animals, and Life Lessons

Lucy Llama and Friends: Short Stories, Fuzzy Animals, and Life Lessons

Ethan the Eagle and Friends; Short Stories, Fuzzy Animals, and Life Lessons

Billy Brown Bear and Friends; Short Stories, Fuzzy Animals, and Life Lessons

Humble Heron and Friends; Short Stories, Fuzzy Animals, and Life Lessons

Peter Penguin and Friends; Short Stories, Fuzzy Animals, and Life Lessons

Other books that we recommend to help children learn important life lessons:

Guaranteed Success for Kindergarten; 50 Easy Things You Can Do Today! by Marrae Kimball

Guaranteed Success for Grade School; 50 Easy Things You Can Do Today! by Marrae Kimball

The Secret Combination to Middle School: Real Advice from Real Kids, Ideas for Success, and Much More! by Marrae Kimball

Again, thank you for reading and sharing this book! YOU are making the world a better place. Please consider leaving a short review as it helps us spread the message! Children deserve the very best that life offers. All children deserve a chance at a successful and happy life.

If you have ideas for stories, please feel free to share and send them to:

Melissa Eshleman
Find Your Way Publishing, Inc.
PO Box 667
Norway, ME 04268
Melissa@findyourwaypublishing.com

www.findyourwaypublishing.com

Thank you!

Disclaimer